THE SHORT STORIES OF
GRACE LIVINGSTON HILL

THE SHORT STORIES

OF

GRACE LIVINGSTON HILL

Edited by

J. E. CLAUSS

The American Reprint Company

NEW YORK
1976

FIRST EDITION

Copyright © 1976 by J.E. Clauss

Portions of this book are republished
by Special Arrangement with J.B. Lippincott Com,

Library of Congress Catalog Card Number 76-430
International Standard Book Number 0-89190-101-9

AMERICAN REPRINT, a division of
The American Reprint Company/Rivercity Press
Box 476
Jackson Heights, New York 11372

Manufactured in the United States of America
by Inter-Collegiate Press, Inc. Mission, Kansas

THE SHORT STORIES OF GRACE LIVINGSTON HILL

FOREWORD

Few American story tellers have had the continued popularity of Grace Livingston Hill.

Mrs. Hill wrote her first story at the age of ten and continued writing until her death in 1947. Her novels have sold an estimated eight million copies in hard cover and continue to captivate readers across the Americas to this day.

In her delightful and charming romances, there remains a constant positive spirit that conquers discouragement, and supports that true love and happiness are born from the worst of trials. Her gift is of understanding—making her characters seem real and her stories true to life.

For nearly 44 years the stories contained in this volume were lost. When they first appeared in 1932 under the imprint of the J. B. Lippincott Co., each story was bound separately. Because they were originally very small volumes, they probably were lost amongst the proliferation of works during the Depression. Most likely, they were not reprinted due to the fact that only one or two copies of each were ever found.

These short stories appear in the original order of publication with the hope that the fans of Grace Livingston Hill will enjoy this and the other two volumes planned for publication.

J. E. Clauss
Camelot, Mass., 01337
January, 1976

BEGGARMAN

by

GRACE LIVINGSTON HILL

Beggarman

Time: Middlemorning of a
sunny Spring day.
Place: Fifth Avenue.

The air is drifting full of the breath of hyacinths and daffodils from the near-by flower shops. People are wearing spring blossoms in their buttonholes. A general atmosphere of happiness and keen relish of life is in the faces that pass.

Around a corner a blind beggar creeps along, a look of purpose in his sightless countenance, tapping laboriously ahead of him on the walk with a stout wooden cane. Approaching from the uptown direction comes a girl with glints of gold in her hair, and a discontented look about her rather pretty mouth. She wears a rich but simple spring costume and a large bunch of fresh violets that match her eyes. She is not enjoying the spring sunshine nor the scent of the hyacinths. Her gaze is far away, straight over the head of the blind beggar whom she notices no more than a mote in the sunshine.

THE CANE. "Tap! Tap! Tap! A hollow sound! Tap! Tap! *Steps* to the right! Broad low steps! Many of them! Yes, steps. Wide steps!"

BLIND BEGGAR (Pausing and swinging the cane to the right till it touches the rise of the first step, then tapping along its edge). "Yes, steps."

THE CANE (On the walk again). "Tap! Tap! A lady close at hand!"

BLIND BEGGAR (Looking up and listening). "Lady, is this a church? Lady, will you help me up those steps? I am blind."

THE GIRL (Shrinking back). "Why do you want to go to church?"

BLIND BEGGAR. "Because I have only another day to live. There are things that I must do."

THE GIRL. "How do you know that? You have not been condemned to death, have you?"

BLIND BEGGAR. "Condemned? Yes—condemned. Condemned to death; but not by the law of the land."

THE GIRL. "I might die tomorrow too. Anybody might. No one knows. But it isn't likely."

BLIND BEGGAR (Turning his sightless eyes impressively toward her). "There is a doctor down in the miserable hole where we herd at night. He told me I had twenty-four hours to live if I saved my strength. *I have not saved my strength!* It is going fast! I have come a long way since sunrise."

THE GIRL. "Your doctor was likely mistaken. I will call an ambulance. You should go to a hospital, not a church."

BLIND BEGGAR. "No, the doctor was not mistaken. He was a famous doctor once, before he let go his grip on himself. He *knows*—and *I* know! and I must go to the church before it is too late. If you are afraid, Lady, or in haste, I will try to go by myself. Just count the steps for me and say if the door is open, and I will not hinder you."

THE GIRL (With sudden determination). "No, I am not afraid, nor in haste. Come, we will go. Lay your hand on my arm. Now turn so—lift your foot. It is not a long flight.—But you look ill—you are short of breath! I do not think you ought to go!"

BLIND BEGGAR (Determinedly). "I go!"

THE GIRL (Looking up ahead as they mount). "There are beautiful carved bronze doors. It is a pity you cannot see them."

BLIND BEGGAR (Eagerly). "How are they, Lady, closed and fast?"

THE GIRL. "No, one is standing wide. A woman just came out looking as if she had been praying."

BLIND BEGGAR (Excitedly). "Oh, then it is not too late!"

THE GIRL (Curiously). "Why are you so anxious to get to the church? It is much pleasanter out here in the sunshine. In there it is dark and cheerless."

BLIND BEGGAR. "Because I am a great sinner. It is for this cause I am blind and poor and a beggar. I have only a little time left. If one could find God anywhere it seems as if it ought to be in a church. Lady—I was not always blind and poor—and a beggar. I was once young and good and happy as you are."

THE GIRL. "I am not happy. I am not sure that I'm so very good—!"

BLIND BEGGAR. "Be happy and be good then while yet there is time. I started just that way one day,—and look at me now! What whim of fancy clouds your life? Some priceless bauble you can't have? Or does the round of pleasure pall upon you? You are a child of fortune, I'll be bound. One touch of your soft sleeve tells me the tale. I know good cloth when I can touch it, yet,—though 'tis many years since any came my way. But why should one like you be unhappy? Are *you* blind? Are *you* a sinner? Are *you* dying to-morrow?"

THE GIRL (Shuddering). "Come, this is the last step and then we are within. Shall I lead you to a seat and leave you to rest awhile? I could find someone from the hospital and send him to you."

BLIND BEGGAR (Groping). "So this is the house of God! Let me touch the wall. How wide and high it seems. No, Lady, do not leave me yet. You are unhappy; stay, and find some healing for your trouble, too."

THE GIRL. " 'Tis not a matter with which to trouble a God. 'Tis only a poor man that I love, and one with money that I cannot love, and I a pawn between the two. 'Tis nothing, I suppose, beside the troubles of a universe."

BLIND BEGGAR (Laughing bitterly to himself). "Ha! Ha! 'Rich man, poor man, beggarman, thief!' *My son* is a *thief!* We have all the others down there where I've been,—'doctor, lawyer, merchant, chief!' The Chief of Police! Ha! Ha! You know the old nursery rhyme. They counted it out on their buttons, and on the petals of flowers, little girls with innocent laughing eyes, and no idea what any of the names meant. They never knew what *Sin* was, those children! There was one, a little girl with eyes like blue flowers that I sinned against, and dragged down—! and *my son*— HE IS A THIEF! But ——" (in a whisper) "it-is-not-all-his-fault!"

THE GIRL (Shrinking back frightened into the shadows). "Oh, I must go! I will give you some money and go!"

BLIND BEGGAR. "No, Lady, I want no money! I am done with begging! What is money when one is about to die? There is help in this house somewhere, and you must lead me to it. I know it is here for my mother believed it and taught it to me. I always knew back in my soul it was true, and that it would come out in my last hour and haunt me. Come, let us go a little farther in!" (Laying his hand heavily upon her shoulder like a command). "Look up, Lady! Is God anywhere here? Can you see Him?"

THE GIRL (Lifting fearful eyes under her modish little hat and hesitating—). "There are pictures about on the stained glass windows."

BLIND BEGGAR (Eagerly). "Pictures! What pictures?"

THE GIRL. "There is one of a man bearing a heavy beam across his back—a cross— It is a cross! And there are many following in a crowd with stones in their hands and menace in their eyes. They hate Him and would like to kill Him."

BLIND BEGGAR (Thoughtfully). "What is His face like? —The face of the one bearing the Cross?"

THE GIRL. "It is full of tenderness like one who loved greatly and was suffering for that love. It seems strange, but it is almost as if the love in His face were for those who were persecuting Him. He seems more like a God than a man."

Blind Beggar (Convincingly). "It is Jesus Christ the Son of God as my mother used to teach me! I know the story well. Let us kneel here in the aisle, for my strength is going fast. I will hold to the end of the pew. Now, look again and tell me. You say there is a crowd about Him? What sort of a crowd?"

The Girl. "A mob! A rabble of all sorts! And yet— there are women among them too, and little children, some even so small they are carried."

Blind Beggar. "Look carefully and tell me; is there one among them all that *looks like ME*? See! I will lift up my face to the light of the ceiling! Now, look quick and tell me if I am among those who persecuted Him. Are you looking?"

The Girl (Kneeling, with white uplifted face from among the shadows of the dim aisle, studying the ghastly anxious face of the blind beggar, and then searching among the painted faces of the crowd on the window). "I—am—looking ——"

Blind Beggar. "Hurry! Have you found me? Tell me quick! I cannot bear it."

The Girl (With a sharp catch in her throat and

the breath of a sob). "They—are—only painted faces ——!"

BLIND BEGGAR. "You have found me? is it so? I was among those who followed Him to His death?—who caused His death? Oh,—*My God!* I *knew* it! I knew it all the time!—Yet I went on—! Tell me,—is it not so?"

THE GIRL (Evasively). "It is only a painting, you know. It was not meant for you."

BLIND BEGGAR (With bowed head). "But it *is* me! You recognized me! Yes,—the guilt is mine! What madness to suppose there is any hope for such as I. But— you are silent! *You have not gone away and left me?*" (Groping toward the girl with one hand). "Why,— you are weeping! Is it worse than even I had guessed? Tell me quick! Was it I who struck Him? Or gathered thorns to pierce His brow? Or helped to lift Him on the cross? Oh, tell me quick and put an end to my misery!"

THE GIRL (Catching her breath in a sob and wiping away the tears that gather). "No, no,—you are just one of the crowd. It was not that. It was not you at all

that wrung my heart. It was—that I have—found—
my—own—face—there!—with such a scorn, and such
a look of pride and self-conceit, like one who never
thinks of any but herself! Oh—can I be like that?
And—*did He know?*"

BLIND BEGGAR (Excitedly, panting, great drops of per-
spiration standing on his pale forehead). "Don't weep!
Let us do something! The time is getting short. I must
find someone to help. Are there no more windows?"

THE GIRL (Lifting her streaming eyes to the opposite
wall). "There is another beyond. They are lifting Him
on the Cross. One nails His hands. Oh——!" (Stifling
a cry and sinking down with her face in her hands.)

BLIND BEGGAR (Desperately). "What is it? Are we there
too?"

THE GIRL (With muffled despairing voice). "We are
there."

BLIND BEGGAR (Wildly, flinging out his hands). "Look
again! Find another picture quick! The time is going.
Look over there." (He points vacantly to the other
side of the church.)

THE GIRL (Turning in the direction he is pointing). "I

see three crosses." (Wearily) "They are on the hill-top, and three figures hang on them. The sky is darkening and the crowd draws back. I cannot see the faces of the crowd—but—*we are there*——!"

BLIND BEGGAR (Eagerly). "Wait! I remember the rest of the story. There were two thieves on those other two crosses, and one He *forgave*! Let us go to the altar and ask for mercy! Come!" (The Beggar struggles to his feet by the aid of the pew end and his cane which he still grasps.)

THE CANE. "Tap! Tap! Tap!" (A hollow sound over the tessellated marble echoing into the vaulted ceiling, strangely out of place, and stirring the quiet from little dark shadows in the frescoes) "Tap! Tap! Tap! We are nearing something in front. Tap!" (Warningly) "There are steps ahead!"

BLIND BEGGAR. "Is this the altar?"

THE GIRL (Looking intently ahead). "Yes, this is the altar. Shall we kneel?"

BLIND BEGGAR (Dropping painfully upon his knees with his hand resting on the old cane). "Now, if He be near,—" (His sightless eyes peer wistfully ahead.)

THE CANE (Slipping and rolling to the floor with a wooden ring like a cry of awe). "There is some One standing before you with His hands outstretched ——!"

BLIND BEGGAR (Pleadingly, with clasped hands and sightless eyes lifted). "Be merciful to me a sinner!——"

THE GIRL (Dropping beside him on one knee with bowed head and clasped hands drooping at one side, her voice almost a whisper). "And to me also ——!" (The two remain kneeling motionless with bowed heads.)

THE ORGAN (Stealing softly, almost inaudibly into the silence, and swelling into distinctness like a healing tide of sound).

"Depth of mercy, can there be,
Mercy still reserved for me?"

(The music softly dies away again into the silence.)

BLIND BEGGAR (With eyes fixed as on some One close at hand, and a glorified look of worship and pleading on his worn pale face). "Be merciful ——!"

THE GIRL (Still with closed eyes and intent drooping figure, murmuring earnestly). "—to *me*—a *sinner!*"

THE CHOIR (Breaking forth with assurance).

> "There's a wideness in God's mercy,
> Like the wideness of the sea. . . .
> . . . There is mercy with the Saviour,
> There is healing in His blood."

BLIND BEGGAR (With lifted head and eager face). "Me? A sinner?"

THE GIRL (Softly). "Yes,—a sinner!"

THE ORGAN AND CHOIR (Triumphantly).

> "There is a fountain filled with blood,
> Drawn from Immanuel's veins,
> And sinners plunged beneath that flood
> Lose all their guilty stains."

(As the melody hushes a long beam of jewelled light reaches down through the silence from a costly window above and lays many-colored fingers upon the bowed heads of the Beggar and the Maid.

THE CHOIR (Chanting). "Go—in—peace! A-m-e-n!"

(The two at the altar remain motionless for a moment, then slowly rise.)

BLIND BEGGAR (Groping for his cane). "Come, let us go. It may not be too late even yet."

THE GIRL (Wonderingly). "Where must we go?"

BLIND BEGGAR (Impatiently). "To bring my son who is a thief."

THE GIRL. "But why?"

BLIND BEGGAR. "Why do you have to ask? Do you not understand? I must bring my son to Him! Did you not see HIM at the altar? You, who are not blind at all, did you not *see* Him? Why, I saw Him with my blind eyes, even! Did you not *know* He was there?"

THE GIRL. "Yes, I felt Him in my heart. He touched me on the brow. I know that He forgave me."

BLIND BEGGAR (Eagerly). "And now ——?"

THE GIRL. "And now—all will be different. I go back to ——"

BLIND BEGGAR (Understandingly). "You go back to bring the rich man, and the poor man, I suppose, that they, too, may understand and be healed?"

THE GIRL (Thoughtfully). "I shall *tell* the rich man,—but the poor man I shall *bring with me*—back to His altar."

BLIND BEGGAR. "Farewell then, and blessings on you, little sister, for leading a blind beggar to the Light!" (They part in the bright sunshine of the noon on the flower-scented Avenue. The Girl hastens back uptown, the Blind Beggar turns downtown, tapping along, block after block, panting with shortness of breath.)

BLIND BEGGAR. "If I can only hold out ——!"

THE CANE. "Tap! Tap! Tap! A curb! Tap! Beware! A car!—STEP BACK! No, F O R W A R D!—Alas!! My M-a-s-t-e-r! Oh-h!"

POLICEMAN. "Look aloive there mon! Whut 'r ye doin' ——? Goin' ahid whin me sign's down? Stand asoid iverybody!"

THE CROWD (Jostling, gasping, writhing out of the way, and closing in curiously about the scene again). "Ohh-h! Ahh-h! O-hhhhh!"

A WOMAN (Screaming). "Someone is hurt! Take me away quickly! I am fainting ——!"

POLICEMAN (Waving his club). "Stand asoid iverybody!"

ANOTHER WOMAN (Curiously). "Oh,—who is it? Let me look! It might be somebody I know ——"

POLICEMAN (With a shrug). "Only an ould beggarmaun, laidy. He's croaked fur shure! Git me an ambulance, b'y, an' be quick about it! This strrreet cawn't be blocked."

THE CANE (Rolling into the gutter, kicked, trampled, snapping in two). "Alas,—my M-a-s-t-e-r—! And now—*who will go to bring his son who is a thief* ——?"

The Story of

THE LOST STAR

by
GRACE LIVINGSTON HILL

*The Story of
the Lost
Star*

$\mathcal{A}$BOUT a week before Christmas in a small city of the East there appeared in the Lost and Found column this advertisement:

Lost. Sometime between the World War and the present morning, The Star of Bethlehem. The finder will confer everlasting favor and receive a reward of ten thousand dollars if returned to the owner between the hours of sundown and midnight on Christmas eve.

(Signed) George K. Hamilton,
Eleven, Harvard Place.

The type-setter blinked and paused in his busy work,

read it again and wondered. Ten thousand dollars! Was it a joke? It must be a mistake! But no, it was paid for. It must go in. He punched away at his machine and the lines appeared in the type, but his thoughts were busy. Ten thousand dollars! With that he could, with self respect, marry Mary! He would not have been John if he had not thought of that first.

George K. Hamilton. That was the rich guy who lived in the big house, with one blind wall stuck on its side that everybody said was a picture gallery. He was rolling in wealth so it must be real. But what was this thing he had lost that was worth everlasting favor and ten thousand dollars? A jewel? A silver tablet? Something of intrinsic historic value perhaps? Something that must be well known, or the writer would not have spoken of it in that off-hand indefinite way as *the* Star of Bethlehem, as if there were but one. Bethlehem —Bethlehem—that was the place where they made steel! Steel! Why—steel of course. George K. Hamilton. Hamilton the steel king! Ah! Why hadn't he thought of it at once?

And why couldn't he go to Bethlehem and find out

all about it? He was the first one, excepting the editor of the Lost and Found column, to see this ad. Why wouldn't he stand first chance of the reward if he worked it right?

To be sure there was a possibility that someone, who knew just what this star was, would be able to get on its track sooner, but if he caught the first train in the morning he would have a good start before anyone read the morning papers.

He would be through with his work by three a.m. at the latest, and there was a train at five. He would have time to get back to his boarding place and clean up a bit, perhaps scribble a note to Mary telling her to be ready for the wedding.

His fingers flew over the keys of his machine as he laid his plans, and his heart throbbed with excitement over the great opportunity that had flung its open door right in his humble path. Ten thousand dollars!

Early dawn saw him dressed in his best and hurrying on his way to Bethlehem amid a train load of laborers going out for the day's work. But he saw not pick nor shovel nor dinner pail, nor noted greasy overalls and sleepy-eyed companions. Before his shining eyes was a star, sometimes silver, sumptuously engraved, sometimes gold and set in sparkling jewels, leading him on into the day of adventure.

He essayed to question his fellow seatmate about that star:

"You live in Bethlehem? Did you ever see the Star of Bethlehem?"

But the man shook his head dumbly:

"Me no spak L'angla!"

Arrived in the City of Steel he went straight to the news agent:

"Have you been here some time?"

"Born here."

"Then tell me, have you a Star of Bethlehem?"

The agent shook his head.

"Don't smoke that kind. Don't keep that kind. Try the little cigar store down the street." And he swung himself under the shelf and, shouldering a pile of morning papers, rushed off down the platform.

Out in the street John stopped a man whose foot was just mounting the running board of his car:

"Do you know anything about the Star of Bethlehem?"

"Never heard of it, Man. A Ford's good enough for me!" and he swung into his car and shot away from the curb hurriedly.

He asked a little girl who was hurrying away from the bakery with a basket of bread.

"Why, Star-of-Bethlehem is a flower," she said, "a little green and white starry flower with pointed petals. It grows in the meadow over there in the summer time, but it's all gone now. You can't find Stars-of-Bethlehem this time of year!" And she stared after him for a silly fool.

He asked a passer on the street:

"Can you tell me how to find out about Star of Bethlehem?"

The man tapped him lightly on the shoulder with a wink and advised him knowingly, with a thumb pointing down a side alley:

"You better not mention that openly, brother. There's been several raids around here lately and the police are wise. It ain't safe."

And about this time the Bishop back at home was opening the morning paper at the breakfast table as he toyed with his grapefruit and coffee:

"Ha, ha!" he said as his eye traveled down the column idly and paused at the Lost and Found, "Listen to this, Bella. Poor old George has got 'em again. He probably thinks he is going to die this time. I'll just step in and have a little talk on theology with him this morning and set his mind at rest. No need for that ten thousand dollars to go out of the church. We might as well have it as some home for the Feeble Minded."

Bella left her coffee and came around to read the advertisement, her face lighting intelligently:

"Oh, Basil! Do you think you can work it?" she cried delightedly.

"Why, sure, he's just a little daffy on religion now because he's been sick. The last time I saw him he asked me how we could know any of the creeds were true when they were all so different. I'll smooth it all out for him, and make him give another ten thousand or so to the Social Service work of our church, and he'll come across handsomely, you'll see. I'd better go at once. It won't do to wait, there are too many kinds of crooks on the lookout for just such a soft ten thousand as this." And he took his hat and coat and hurried out.

The Professor at his meagre breakfast table, worrying about his sick wife, and how he could afford to keep his eldest son in college, happened on the item.

He set down his coffee cup untasted and stepped to his book shelves taking down several wise treatises on Astronomy.

A sweet faced saint in an invalid chair read and pondered and murmured thoughtfully: "Poor soul! What's happened to the man's Bible?"

Before night the one little shop in the city that made a specialty of astronomical instruments had been drained of everything in the shape of a searcher of the heavens, and a rush order had gone on to New York by telegraph for more telescopes of various sizes and prices, while a boy in the back office who was good at lettering was busy making a copy of the advertisement to fasten up in the plate glass window, with special electric lights playing about it and a note below:

"Come in and order your telescope now before they

are all gone, and get into line for the great sky prize! We have 'em! All prices!"

Far into the evening the crowd continued around that window and many who had glasses at home hurried away to search for them, and build air castles of how they would spend the ten thousand dollars when they got it.

Even before the day was half over the office of the University was besieged by eager visitors come to question wise ones, a folded newspaper furtively held under each applicant's arm.

As evening drew on shadowy figures stole forth to high places and might have been seen scanning the heavens, and now and then consulting a book by means of a pocket flash light. More than one young student worked into the small hours of the night with reference books scattered about him, writing a many-paged treatise on the Star of Stars, some to prove that the star was a myth, and others that it was still in existence and would one day appear again as bright as of old. Even the police, coming suddenly upon lurking star-gazers far toward morning, began to question what had taken hold of the town.

Coming home on the late train from a fruitless search for an unknown quantity which was not there, John Powers sat wearily back in the fusty seat of the common car and took out the worn advertisement from his pocket to read it once more.

The lost Star of Bethlehem! What could it be? He had searched the steel city from end to end without finding so much as a trace of tradition or story about a star in connection with that town. He had met with more rebuffs and strange suggestions than ever before in his life together, and he was dog-weary and utterly discouraged. If only he had not written that hopeful letter to Mary in the morning!

Now perhaps she would already be planning to have the wedding soon, and where was the money coming from to provide the little home?

Of course it just might happen that after all the star had been lost up in the city, else why should the advertisement have been put in the city paper and not in the Bethlehem local? But even so he had hoped great things from this trip to Bethlehem and now he had only wasted a day and the car fare, and had gotten nowhere at all.

At a local station a loud mouthed traveler got off,

leaving his recent seatmate without anyone to talk to,
and presently he joined John Powers and entered into
conversation, being one of those men who is never
happy unless his tongue is wagging. In the course of
their talk, John found himself asking the old question
again:

"You say you are from Bethlehem? Did you ever hear
of a star in connection with that town? Was there any
memorial tablet or monument or emblem or anything
in the shape of a star, that has been stolen away? Star
of Bethlehem it was called, do you know anything
about it?"

The stranger stared blankly and shook his head:

"Sounds to me as if it might be a song, or a book
mebbe. If you knowed who wrote it you might find out
at one o' the schools. My Johnny says you can find out
almost anything if you know who wrote it. Ever been a
Mason? Might be some kind of a Masonic badge,
mightn't it?"

The man got out at the next station and Powers
leaned back wearily and thought how he had failed. His
mind seemed too tired to think any longer on the subject.

An old lady in a queer bonnet with many bundles at her feet and a basket beside her out of which stuck a pair of turkey's feet, leaned over suddenly and touched him on the shoulder:

"Laddie, hae ye tried the auld Buik?" she asked timidly, "I'm thinkin' ye'll find it all there."

"I beg your pardon!" said Powers lifting his hat courteously and thinking how the blue of her eyes had a light like that in Mary's eyes.

He arose from his seat and went back to sit beside her. Then somehow the blue of her eyes made him unafraid, and he told her all about the ten thousand dollars and his fruitless trip to Bethlehem.

"Oh, but laddie, ye're on the wrong track entirely," said the old lady. "The Star o' Bethlehem's in the auld Buik. I ken it's no the fashion to read it these days, but the worruld lost sight of a lot besides the things it wanted to forget when it set out to put its Bibles awa! Hunt up yer Mither's Bible, lad, and study it out. The star arose in the East ye ken, and the folks who saw it first was those that was lookin' fer its arisin'. The star's na lost. It led to the little King ye ken, an' it'll always lead to the King if a body seeks with all the heirt, fer that is the promise: 'An' ye shall find me, when ye shall seek fer Me with all yer heirts.' May like the puir buddy who wrote the bit lines in the paper was longin' fer the King hisself an' wanted the star to guide him, but ye ken ye can't purchase the gifts of God wi' silver ner gold. The mon may lay his ten thousand baubles at the fut of the throne, but he'll find he must go his own self across the desert, and wait mayhap, before he'll ever see the shinin' of the Star. But you'll not turn back yerself now you've started, laddie! Go find the King fer yerself. Look in the Gospels an' read the story. It's passin' wonderful an' lovely. This is my station now, and I'll be leavin' ye, but it'll be a glad Christmas time fer you ef you find the little King, an' *ye'll find Him* sure, if ye seek on with all yer heirt."

The doorway to the fine old Hamilton mansion on Harvard Place was besieged from morning to night all that week by aspirants wishing to speak with the Master, but to all the grave and dignified servitor who answered the door replied:

"My master is away. He cannot speak with you until

the time appointed. If any then have found the lost treasure they may come and claim the reward. But they must come bringing it with them. None others need present themselves."

Even the Bishop had not been able to gain admittance. He was much annoyed about it. He was afraid others would get ahead of him. He had written a letter, but he knew it had not yet been opened for the last time he called he had seen it lying on the console in the hall with a lot of other unopened letters. The Bishop was very certain that if he could have audience *first* all would be well. He was sure he could explain the philosophy of life and the mystery of the star quite satisfactorily and soothingly.

Before John Powers had gone back to work that night of his return from Bethlehem, he had gone to the bottom of an old chest and hunted out his mother's Bible. It was worn and dropping apart in places, but he put it tenderly on his bed, and following an impulse, dropped to his knees beside it, laying his lips against its dusty covers. Somehow the very look of the old worn covers brought back his childhood days and a sense of sin in that he had wandered so far from the path in which his mother had set his young feet.

All that week he gave all the extra time he had to studying about the star. He did not even go to see Mary. He lost sight of the ten thousand dollars in his interest in the star itself. He was now seeking to find that star for himself, not for the reward that had been offered. He wanted to find the King who was also a Saviour.

The last night before it came time for him to go to his work, he dropped upon his knees once more beside the little tattered book, and prayed:

"Oh Jesus Christ, Saviour of the world, I thank Thee that Thou hast sent Thy star to guide me to Thee. I worship Thee, and I give myself to Thee forever."

* * *

On Christmas eve when the door of the mansion was thrown open a large throng of people entered, and were speedily admitted, one by one, to audience with the master of the house, until, in an incredibly short space of time, the waiting room was emptied of philosophers and dreamers and ambitious ones. Even the Bishop had been courteously sent his way. Only three were left. Three wise ones, and two of them were women!

One was an old woman with a burr upon her tongue and a Bible in her hand; one was a young girl with blue starry eyes and a bit of a Testament in the folds of her gown where she kept her fingers between the leaves to a place. The third was John Powers, standing within the shadow of a heavy curtain beside a deepset window looking out at the great shining of a bright star, with peace upon his face. He turned about as the door closed after the Bishop and glanced at the two women. The girl looked up and their eyes met.

"Mary!"

"John!"

There was scarcely time to recognize the old woman before the door opened and George K. Hamilton, keen of eye, sharp of feature, eager of expression, walked in and looked from one to the other searching each face questioningly.

The young man stepped forward to meet him and Mary saw for the first time that a worn little Bible was in his hand.

But John was speaking in such a ringing voice of certainty:

"Sir, I want to tell you first that I have not come for your money. When I began this search it was in hope of the reward, but I've found the Star itself, and it led me to the King, and now I've brought it to you because I want you to have it too. You'll find it in this Book. It has to be searched for, but it's there. And when you have found it I've been thinking you'll maybe want to sell all that you have and give to the poor and go and follow *Him*. But *I* am not one of those poor any longer, for I *have found the King*! Come, Mary, shall we go?"

Then up rose the old Scotch woman from her place near the door:

"I've just one more word to say, an' ye'll find it in yon Buik: 'Arise, shine; for thy light is come, and the Glory of the Lord is risen upon thee.' That star isn't lost, sir, an' never was! Never will be! It's up in the heavens waiting till the King has need of it again, and some day it will burst upon the world again and they will all know that it has been there all the time!"

* * *

The Master was left alone in his mansion with the book in his hand and a strange awed feeling of the Presence of God in his room.

He looked wonderingly, doubtfully, down at the book, and then wistfully out through his richly draped window to where a single star shone softly through the Christmas night.

HER WEDDING GARMENT

by

GRACE LIVINGSTON HILL

Her
Wedding
Garment

MARTHA WORTH came out of her house one afternoon in early spring, hesitated a moment on the doorstep, looking up and down the street for a taxi, and then decided to walk. At the last minute her car had developed engine trouble. If she waited for repairs she would be late to her various appointments. She hated to be late. She prided herself that she had so systematized everything about her that her life moved as on oiled wheels.

She was meticulously dressed. Every item of her costume was carefully considered and in perfect harmony with every other detail. Martha was always ready with her garments for each changing season as they came.

Her dress was just the right shade of brown cloth trimmed with flat cream-colored fur, altogether the most correct thing for that season. The chic little hat of imported brown straw with its two creamy gardenias under the tilted lacey brim was most becoming, and exactly matched the smart little brown shoes, as the soft doeskin gloves exactly matched the fur jabot about her neck.

If she had any make-up on her face it was so skillfully applied that even a connoisseur was left in doubt as to whether it was not just natural perfection.

Martha stepped gracefully down the street, fully conscious of her own charming appearance, and more than one woman from car or bus or sidewalk, or even hidden behind a sheltering window drapery along the way, watched her with envious eyes, and longed to be like her.

Inside her dainty purse was a gold mounted tablet on which were written her engagements for the afternoon. She was to read a paper at a missionary meeting at half past two. It contained a careful study of the topography of Mohammedan lands, intricate and accurate statistics of the cost of maintaining missions, and the comparative number of natives Christianized. She had figured to a fraction just how much it cost to Christianize each one. The paper would take twenty minutes to read and she had carefully arranged to have it placed first on the program after the opening exercises that she might slip out and meet her other engagements. She was due at a committee meeting of a charitable organization at three-thirty, and she hoped to be through with that by four. With good management she ought to be able to stop at the orphanage and perhaps drop in to Judge Warren's office to see that poor widow who ought to have a pension, before appearing at the Verlenden-Braithwaite tea for a few minutes. All these engagements fitted well together and her costume was quite right for all. A trifle more than was necessary for the missionary meeting perhaps—there would be only a few quiet plain old ladies there, who would scarcely appreciate the cut of her imported ensemble, the real distinction of her whole outfit. Still that was the beauty of costly simplicity. It did not look out of place anywhere.

As she walked down the pleasant street she was thinking of her plans for the coming week. How well she had arranged them. The dressmakers coming just before the Barnwell wedding in plenty of time to finish her new lace dress. It was a little awkward having had to ask that Mrs. White on Sylvan Avenue to change time with her. But of course Mrs. White wouldn't be going to that wedding.

She turned into the main avenue now where were plenty of taxis but it was only five blocks farther, and she had plenty of time, it was hardly worth while taking a taxi.

But even as she glanced at her wrist watch to make sure, a prankish breeze took liberties with her delicate hat, pulling out the neatly marcelled hair from its precise arrangement about her lovely forehead, and tossing her jabot full in her face.

Martha looked up annoyed and discovered the sky suddenly overcast, and a drop of falling rain romped into her eye. April of course. But how unexpected!

Another and another great drop splashed down. Her new ensemble! Would the cloth spot? She started to run, but the wind caught her on one side and the rain on the other and ran with her. All the taxis seemed to have suddenly fled from the avenue. She cast about for a quick shelter and backed into a convenient doorway.

There were others scurrying for this shelter also, many of them, and they crowded her inside the doors. She found herself in a church entrance with the big audience room just behind her, its doors standing wide and people crowding into the seats. There was a meeting going on, but it was not her church.

People were crowding her more and more. A man closed a dripping umbrella directly over her Paris hat and someone stepped harshly on the toe of her lovely new shoe.

"If you will step inside and take a seat you will not be in danger of getting so wet, Madam," said another man in a damp overcoat. Martha retreated into the far corner of a back seat.

Suddenly the audience burst forth into music, and the gladness of it was almost annoying.

> "Jesus may come to-day,
> Glad Day! Glad Day!—"

She shuddered involuntarily as she drew back into her

corner under the gallery. What a startling, unpleasant thought to be flung into the orderliness of her spring day! It was unseemly, singing of the Lord in this familiar way. What a cataclysmic thing it would be to have Christ return to earth in the midst of the everyday work and program. How upsetting! She put the idea away with distaste.

The man who prayed seemed almost too intimate with God. Who were these people? Some peculiar cult that had hired the church for a conference, perhaps?

They burst into song again, every word distinct and clear:

> "He is coming again! He is coming again!
> This very same Jesus, rejected of men ——"

There it was again, another hymn on that same theme! Could it be just a happening? But no, they were reading the scripture:

"In a moment, in the twinkling of an eye, at the last trump ——"

Was it possible that anybody really took those words literally? *Now? To-day?* How incongruous!

What was this meeting into which she had stumbled? A fanatical convention? She looked about the audience room, crowded now to overflowing. There were many people whom she knew, people of wealth and culture, some from her own church. Why! There was Judge Warren up toward the front of the church! And there was Mary, her dear friend! Mary was a saint. Mary was not a fanatic. Could it be that Mary believed such queer things, or had she, too, come in just for shelter from the rain?

Her meditations were arrested by a strong tender voice from the platform:

"We know that our Lord Jesus is coming back to earth in visible form, first because He said He would: 'Let not your heart be troubled . . . If I go and prepare a place for you I will come again, and receive you unto myself.' "

Martha sat up startled and began to listen, an anxious little frown between her eyes. She had earned a Testament at the age of five for learning this fourteenth chapter of John, but never had she dreamed it had any reference to a literal return of the Lord. Outside the rain was pouring down but she did not hear it. She was listening to this strange new doctrine. In all the years of her placid church-going twice a Sunday she had never heard this doctrine preached before! Was it something new? Did people generally believe it? Passage of scripture, words and phrases that suggested a possible coming of some One in the dim and misty future ages she had always looked upon as figures of speech, fantastic picture language.

"The angels testified that Jesus would come again," said the speaker. " 'This same Jesus which is taken from you, up into heaven, shall so come in like manner as ye have seen Him go into heaven.'

"And Paul gave his testimony later: 'In a moment, in the twinkling of an eye, at the last trump: for the trumpet shall sound, and the dead shall be raised incorruptible, and we shall be changed.' "

Martha shuddered, but the clear voice went steadily on repeating strangely familiar words that had never meant a thing to her before:

" 'For the Lord Himself shall descend from heaven with a shout, with the voice of the archangel, and with the trump of God: and the dead in Christ shall rise first: then we which are alive and remain shall be caught up together with them in the clouds, to meet the Lord in the air; and so shall we ever be with the Lord. Wherefore comfort one another with these words.' "

Martha caught nothing of the comfort that these words were meant to be. She heard only the announcement of what to her seemed a catastrophe for which she was unprepared. She sat up sharply and listened with a startled pink spot glowing on each cheek as the verses multiplied. The man was actually stating that one out of every twenty-five verses in the New Testament referred to the return of the Lord. Surely that could not be so or she would have heard other ministers preaching about it. Could this one be right and all the others wrong?

The speaker went on to unfold prophecy. Martha had never heard before that the fig tree in the Bible always typified the Jewish people as a nation. She listened in amazement as the speaker reminded his audience that Jesus, when questioned of the times and seasons, had told His disciples that when they should see the fig tree putting forth leaves they were to know that His coming was close at hand. Surely this was far fetched, she thought, to take this symbolic language literally and think that it had any reference to the present day effort of the Jews to establish in Palestine a national home. The speaker even dared to state that one of the main reasons for the world war was that Palestine might be once more in hands friendly to the Jews. He reminded his hearers that as soon as this was accomplished the war stopped.

Martha cast a hasty indignant glance about to see how the rest of the audience received this startling statement about the great world war where all the dear boys died to make the world safe for democracy. Think of all those bronze tablets everywhere, and the marble triumphal arches bearing the names of heroes, all the knitting, and the Red Cross bandages, and going without sugar in coffee, just to give Palestine back to the Jews! Ridiculous! An impertinence! Surely someone would get up and protest at this. But everyone was listening in eager absorption. Even her friend Mary wore a look of rapt exaltation.

And now Martha's attention was caught again. In quick succession, like spirits out of the past, came other proofs of the near approach of the great event, history written hundreds of years in advance, that was being fulfilled to the very letter. The records of fulfillment, many of them, were gathered out of the daily papers, events of which she herself had read. She had already recognized the world-wide tendency toward confederation under one head, found among nations, among corporations, among organizations of every kind. She had, in fact, written a paper recently on that very subject and read it before the current events section of the women's club, for Martha Worth was a well-read, thinking woman, well-known to be up-to-date on politics and international affairs. But this astounding speaker dared to affirm that this tendency must surely lead in time to the coming of a great superman, a world-ruler, who should be none other than the Anti-Christ of the Bible.

Martha had to admit, as she listened to verses of scripture, that the League of Nations had certainly been prophesied. She heard with increasing horror the words concerning the "Prince of Rosh," the ruling spirit of Russia, who would spread terror from the north. She suddenly realized the tremendous significance of the revived importance of Rome. She heard for the first time about the two seasons of rainfall in Palestine, the "former" or early rain, and the "latter" rain late in the year which had ceased long ago "according to the word of the Lord," causing desolation in the land. She heard the prophecy read that it would surely not return until the Lord's approach was near; heard how it had most amazingly returned within recent years, only a few drops the first year, a little more the second, until now it had attained its normal fall, making a great change in the fertility of the land, "according to the word of the Lord."

With bated breath, sitting far forward in her seat, utterly unmindful of the rain outside, or of her unfulfilled engagements, she listened to those astonishing words of Paul writing to Timothy:

"This know also, that in the last days perilous times shall come. For men shall be lovers of their own selves, covetous, boasters, proud, blasphemers, disobedient to parents, unthankful, unholy, without natural affection, trucebreakers, false accusers, incontinent, fierce, despisers of those that are good, traitors, heady, highminded, lovers of pleasures more than lovers of God; having a form of godliness, but denying the power thereof."

Instance after instance of the fulfillment of these things occurred to Martha as she listened with troubled, unbelieving eyes fixed upon the speaker, while he made clear how these words fitted the present time.

And then, education! Increase of knowledge! Mechanical inventions! Airplanes, automobiles! Why, it was extraordinary that the Bible prophecies had held promise of all this throughout the ages and nobody had ever noticed it before!

And lastly she heard about the apostasy of the church. That phrase never had meant a thing to her before. Indeed she doubted if she had ever heard it. Now it seemed blasphemy! She could not believe that the Bible had really said that about the church, the holy church, that it should become apostate! Why, if the church was all wrong what was there left? Surely the church was doing more than ever to-day! She had heard many preachers tell how it was making the world better and better.

But this speaker struck at many of the activities and organizations of the day, that she considered sacred as the Bible and the church itself. She grew indignant. These were the activities that made up her whole life! They were the things upon which she relied to make sure her heavenly calling!

Rapidly the thrilling address drew to a close with wonderful, frightening words of how Christ was coming first to the air to take away the true church, the church that was not apostate. That implied that not all church members, not even all active church members, would belong to the church invisible, the body of Christ, who eventually would be caught up to meet the Lord in the air.

Indignation and fear struggled in her heart as she listened to the description of what would follow the sound of that silver trumpet. The dead arising! Her eyes filled with sudden tears. A kind of horror seized her at the thought of being caught up that way with

the dead!—But they would be *alive!*—and of course she
would not want to be left out if such a thing were really
going to be, if it really had the sanction of well thinking,
right living people of God! Of course she would be one
of those who belonged to the Lord. She had always been
an active Christian worker. Why she had always been
present to teach her Sunday School class, even when she
had been out at a party till two or three o'clock Sunday
morning. Even when she had no time to study her
lesson she had always asked the questions in the lesson
leaf faithfully and told her girls to look them up for
next Sunday when they couldn't answer them. Of course
she didn't always remember to ask if they had, but—
well she had always been faithful to her Sunday School
class.

With the last word of warning, "Watch!" ringing in
her ears she rose with the rest for the closing hymn:

"It may be at morn, when the day is awaking,
  When sunlight through darkness and shadow is
      breaking,
    That Jesus will come in the fullness of glory,

To receive from the world 'His own.'
Oh, Lord Jesus, how long, how long, ere we shout the
glad song,
Hallelujah! Christ returneth!"

Then with a frightened hunger in her soul she turned
reluctantly to go back to her world.

She was halfway home before she remembered her
appointments for the afternoon. The missionary meeting! It would have been over long ago! She looked at
her watch, half past four! She could scarcely believe her
eyes. She held the watch to her ear to make sure it was
still going. Half past four! She had been in that queer
meeting over two hours. The charitable association
would have adjourned at four, and the orphanage visitors' hours would be over too before she could get there.
Judge Warren had been in the meeting so he would
not be in his office and she could not go there. There
was nothing of her afternoon's program left but the tea,
and somehow she felt strangely out of harmony with the
atmosphere of a tea. She had a longing to rush home
to her Bible and try to look up some of those references

the speaker had quoted just to prove they were not there.

Of course it was all a hoax. Some queer kind of new doctrine that would soon be shown up as dangerous and disturbing. She wished she had written down the references, but they would surely be easy to find, they were so odd they would shout at one from the pages. She had a vague notion that one of them was in Job and another in Revelation, and weren't some of them in those queer little books at the end of the Old Testament that one could never find? But she had a concordance somewhere in the library. She would find them.

When she reached home she went to work at once, not even waiting to take off her new hat and coat. She turned the leaves of her Bible rapidly. Revelation caught her eye, and suddenly she halted at a verse. Ah! Here was one they had missed at the meeting, but somehow it had a sinister tone. How had they missed this? "Behold I come as a thief. Blessed is he that watcheth, and keepeth his garments, lest he walk naked, and they see his shame."

A chill went through her. Garments! Would one have to prepare garments for such a time?

Martha had no knowledge of dispensational truth. She was not aware that Christ does not come to His own as a thief, but as a Heavenly Bridegroom. She saw only that awful word, "I come" reiterated and a foreboding filled her.

Turning the leaves rapidly again to the end of the book she came on another verse: "He which testifieth these things saith: Surely, I come quickly! Amen" and then that lilt of an answer—so strange that anyone could feel that way! "Even so, come, Lord Jesus." But of course that was for those who were watching, probably, and had their garments all ready. But she shuddered. That picture of walking naked before the assembled world at such a time was terrible! She must get rid of all these notions immediately. She would go and find Mary and talk it over with her. Mary was sane, and Mary was a saint. Mary would dispel this gloom. She must get into a better frame of mind before Tom came home.

So she put away her Bible and went to Mary's house.

Mary had just come home from meeting and was sitting with her Bible and note book going over the references from the meeting.

Mary greeted her joyously.

"Oh, you were out this afternoon, weren't you? Wasn't it wonderful! I tried to reach you after it was over, but somebody held me up and when I reached the door you were gone."

"Wonderful?" echoed Martha in amazement. "Who is he? What is he? Mary, do you believe all that? Do really nice people believe it?"

"Believe it? You mean believe that Christ is coming soon? Why, of course. It is the blessed hope of Christians, dear. Don't you believe it? It is one of the articles of the faith of our church you know. Most Christians throughout the ages have believed it, haven't they?"

"I'm sure I don't know," said Martha crossly, "I never heard of it before. That is, I never supposed for an instant that anyone took those verses seriously. I never heard a minister preach on it, and I've been going to church regularly since I was a child."

"I know," said Mary sadly. "It does seem as if many

ministers are afraid of it, I wonder why? But lately, dear, I've been hearing it a lot. There have been several other speakers on the subject in the city the last month or two. One from Australia, this one from London, and two men from our own land."

"But do you really mean that you believe all that man said? You think Christ is literally coming to earth—and *soon*?"

"I certainly do!" said Mary with a solemn gladness in her voice and a light in her eyes. "Isn't it glorious!"

Martha studied her friend's face with troubled eyes.

"Well, then," she asked at last with an anxious sigh, "if that is really so, how would one go about getting ready? What would one—*wear* on such an occasion?"

"Oh," laughed Mary happily. "We don't have to worry about that. That's all taken care of. If we are His own, and included in that wonderful affair in the air our garments are all provided for us."

Martha stiffened with dignity.

"What do you mean, provided for us? I couldn't think of accepting a costume for that or any other occasion. No self-respecting person would. It would be like renting a wedding suit. I always believe in preparing for all occasions. A well-ordered life will be prepared for every emergency. My mother always kept a shroud in the house in case of sudden death in the family. But can't you tell me what would be expected? Isn't there something said about it in the Bible? I thought it was very queer he didn't tell how to be prepared."

" 'That I may be found *in Him*'," quoted Mary softly.

"Oh, yes, of course," said Martha sharply, "but I mean, *really*. Don't you know what we are supposed to wear? What is the material?"

"Oh, yes," said Mary quietly, "white linen, of course."

"Linen!" Martha looked annoyed. "You don't really mean linen—*handkerchief* linen, perhaps? But wouldn't that muss awfully?"

"It's *righteousness*, you know," explained Mary gravely.

Martha caught at the word.

"Oh, I see," said she with relief. "Well, that's not so hard. Thank you so much. But I must be getting home.

If this thing is really coming off soon I'll have to get to work."

"But dear," said Mary anxiously, "you don't understand. You don't have to provide a garment. Christ has provided it Himself. He says ——"

"But I tell you I couldn't think of accepting that. It may be well enough for some poor, sick, ignorant, incapable souls, but I take it He expects more of those who have been better taught. Doesn't it say something about working out your own salvation? Good bye, I must hurry. It is almost time for Tom to be home and I have to look over the dinner table to see if the spoons and forks are all on. We have a new maid and she is always making mistakes. Tom does get so upset when the table isn't set right."

Mary stood at the door and watched her friend go down the street, repeating thoughtfully, sorrowfully to herself the words:

"For I bear them record that they have a zeal of God, but not according to knowledge. For they, being ignorant of God's righteousness, and going about to establish their own righteousness, have not submitted themselves unto the righteousness of God. For Christ is the end of the law for righteousness unto every one that believeth."

Martha went home and sat down with her Bible and concordance again, looking up Righteousness. Ah, here was a verse:

"I put on righteousness and it clothed me. My judgment was as a robe and a diadem."

That was comforting. She had always been praised for her good judgment.

And here was another in Revelation:

"For the marriage of the Lamb is come, and his wife hath made herself ready, and to her was granted that she should be arrayed in fine linen, clean and white, for the fine linen is the righteousness of the saints."

So, Mary was right, linen was a symbol of righteousness. And she, Martha, was probably accounted a saint, in the heavenly accounting. Saint Martha! That sounded well.

Martha sat for some minutes looking off into space, thinking over her own virtues, and the many good deeds that were against her name, until when her husband came she arose with a sigh of satisfaction, her gloom all dispelled.

Tom had brought a man home to dinner with him and they had a gay evening together. Martha forgot all about the happenings of the afternoon and her disturbed thoughts. Not until they had retired for the night and the lights were out did she remember anything about it. Suddenly she spoke out in the darkness:

"Tom, did you know there were people who believe that Christ is coming back to earth again?"

"Poppycock!" said Thomas sleepily.

"No, but really Tom. Our church believes it. It's a part of their faith."

"Well, they've kept mighty good and still about it if they do," laughed Thomas. "Where have you been this afternoon? We'll have you putting on a white nightgown and sitting on a fence rail to watch for an opening in the sky pretty soon if you get started on such notions. Don't you know there were a lot of nuts got that in their heads several years ago and went to the dogs over it? Sold all they had and nearly starved to death! Went crazy when it didn't happen the way they had planned! For heaven's sake cut it out! I want to get some sleep!"

Martha said no more but she couldn't stop thinking and she presently began to count over all that she had done to make the world better. Surely she would not lack for material for the right garments. At last she dropped into an uneasy sleep.

Sometime in the night she thought she heard a distant sound, clear, sweet, *peremptory* like a trumpet! She sat up instantly in bed with the thought, "Can that be the trump of God?" It came again, more clearly, and she thought "He is come and I am not ready!" What could she do quickly in this emergency? It was the first time in her life that she had been caught unprepared for any great event.

Then she thought she remembered two chests in the attic, carefully put away from dust and moth. One was labeled "VIRTUES" and the other "GOOD DEEDS." She must get to them quickly and somehow array herself before it was too late, that she should not walk naked and be ashamed.

She thought she took her bedroom candle and crept

softly toward the stairs. She must not waken Tom yet, not till she was sure. She dreaded his sarcasm. If this should turn out not to be the trump of God she would never hear the last of it!

In the dim dusty attic she set down her candle on an old trunk, and opened the chests. First the one labeled VIRTUES. Yes, right there on the very top lay the diadem of her judgment, catching weird rays from the candle light and flinging them back into her sleep-filled eyes. That would be lovely for a coronet. And there was her sweet temper lying next, a placid necklace of pearls. And her Perseverance! That had brought her much praise from the church officers, though her husband would insist on calling it persistence, spelled with a small p. But it would stand her in good stead now, a soft firm garment. Ah, she had accomplished many things for good purposes through that virtue. Next was a bright little gold girdle of Truth, and anklets of church-going on Sabbath, bracelets of kindness, feathers of smiles and pleasant words, oh, there was plenty of material here for adornment.

She turned to the other chest and took out her good

deeds. There was a shining piece of golden silk that stood for adherence to the commandments, inwrought with a ribbon of blue and fringe on the border. Oh, she had kept the letter of the law most scrupulously. And there was a piece of white linen. She seized upon it eagerly. That must be for the outer robe. Its border was made of cunning needlework representing the many things that she had done for church and state. A little intricate design of flowers and faces, and scenes from her life. There for instance was her Sunday School class, bright gay young girls, and the boys who belonged in their crowd. How often she had gathered them for good times, always insisting that it should be in the name of the church, with allegiance to its outward forms. They danced along the border of that linen fabric in gay silk colors, their very expressions portrayed in detail. And then the gay procession merged into a scene more grave. These were the men who had come to her for work when times were hard, the ones she had fed, and helped, the wives and mothers for whom she had found shelter and food and labor, the orphanage for whom she had begged dolls and toys, the members of her charitable organization who had done her homage, the people she had called upon in the every-member canvass; and mingled with them all the flowers she had provided for the church, for the sick, and the sad, a gay garland for the border.

Hark! Was that a nearer trumpet sound? With trembling hands she slipped the garments over her head, threw them quickly about her shoulders, and draped around her waist and shoulders the lengths of broidered white linen, donned necklaces, bracelets, the diadem upon her forehead, slipped her feet into a pair of golden shoes wrought delicately of the adulation of her own small world, and stood ready, listening.

Another peal of silver sound came trembling nearer, and she snatched up an armful of white linen from the chest. Tom would need something at the last minute, and of course would look to her to provide it, blame her perhaps if it was not close at hand.

She stooped to pick up her candle and hurry down the stairs, for the silver sound was coming close now and filled all the dusty attic shadows with a thrilling wonder.

But suddenly a blinding light shone round about her, a light so great that it fairly overwhelmed her. She closed her eyes and could not look at first, but gradually she grew accustomed to the brightness, and knew that it was glory, God's glory. What was it doing here in her attic? Ah, God had seen that she was ready, dressed in her own righteousness. Saint Martha! Her heart swelled with pride! She lifted her head with new courage and looked at the glory. Lo, it was a mirror and herself reflected in it!

With pride she looked with open face to see herself. But—what was this? A poor frightened ghastly face, a gaunt figure draped in tattered, soiled garments, dirty, besmirched, disgusting!

She put a trembling hand down and felt for her linen robe, ran a quivering finger over the broidered border, watching herself in the glass to make sure it was herself she saw. Where were gone the golden threads that were woven so cunningly among the flowers? Tarnished! Blackened! Spoiled! And the flowers were faded, their glorious colors sickly in the glory light! The linen itself was dirty and dropping in tatters! The brightness of

His glory in the room showed all the destruction that she had not seen in the fond satisfaction of her own little candle light.

She looked at her own image more closely now, with failing heart, and saw her very face and hands were thick with soil, the dust of the attic upon her brow, and in sudden humiliation and fear she dropped upon her knees.

Then a Voice spoke, out of the silence and glory:

"All our righteousnesses are as filthy rags!"

The words went through her soul like a sword. She looked again toward the One who seemed to stand there before her, with his glory like a mirror, and saw the sin stains upon herself, saw that the filthy rags were unfit covering in which to appear before the Lord of Glory.

Then a strange thing happened. In the silence of that glory-filled attic, Martha knelt and began to understand that all things for which she had striven, all her former ideals, wishes, ambitions, pride, even her good works and virtues were worth nothing. There was only one thing worth while in the whole world, and that was to know Christ.

Suddenly, out of the memory of her childhood came words that spoke themselves to her very soul again with a new meaning that thrilled her as she had never been thrilled before:

But what things were gain to me, those I counted loss for Christ. Yea, doubtless, and I count all things but loss . . . that I may win Christ, and be found *in* Him, not having mine own righteousness, which is of the law, but that which is through the faith of Christ, the righteousness which is of God by faith."

Then all at once the room was filled once more with the soft silver sound of trumpets, and golden angelic voices began to sing:

"When He shall come with trumpet sound.
Oh, may I then in Him be found!
Dressed in His righteousness alone,
Faultless to stand before His throne.
On Christ the solid rock I stand,
All other ground is sinking sand."

THE HOUSE
ACROSS THE HEDGE

by

GRACE LIVINGSTON HILL

The House
Across
the Hedge

$\mathcal{M}$IRIAM, humming a happy
little tune, hurried about her morning tasks, washing the
dishes, shaking out the cloth and folding it carefully,
sweeping the hearth, and the front door stone.

Occasionally, with glad anticipation in her eyes, she
glanced out of the lattice to the house across the hedge;
the hedge which separated her father's yard from the
handsome grounds of the rich influential Egyptian
whose daughter Zelda was Miriam's dearest friend.

That hedge was also the dividing line between Goshen
where Miriam lived, and the great alluring, glittering
Egypt where Zelda lived; but a hard-beaten path ran

from door to door, and a distinct space in the hedge showed where the children of both houses had been wont to go back and forth from babyhood.

Miriam turned from gazing out the lattice as her mother came in from the garden with a basket of herbs.

"Mother," she said eagerly, "I've finished everything now and I'd like to go over to Zelda's right away. She's giving a party to-night, Mother. A wonderful party. And she's invited Joseph and me. She wanted us to come over this morning and help her prepare."

Miriam's eyes shone like two dark stars. Her mother watched her with growing dismay as she put down her basket.

"Oh, I'm sorry, dear," she said gently, "but you mustn't either of you be away from the house to-day!"

A stormy look came into Miriam's eyes.

"Oh, but Mother, you don't understand! I must go. This isn't just an ordinary party. It's a dance, and there is to be an orchestra from the city, and caterers. A great many people are invited, the sons and daughters of officers high in authority. It is a great honor that we are invited. And you needn't worry about having to get me a new dress to wear. Zelda is going to lend me a lovely new one of her own, green and gold with crimson threads in the border. It just fits me and I look wonderful in it. There is a gold chain, and armlets and anklets of gold to wear with it, and Balthazar is getting me flowers from a real florist's to wear in my hair. He said to me:

"'You will be the prettiest girl at my sister's party.' He has asked me to dance with him. Really, Mother, don't you see I must go? And Zelda's father has been so kind to my father, putting him into a better position, it wouldn't do to offend them."

"Miriam, I'm so sorry dear child!" said her mother steadily, "but we are having a solemn feast to-night. God has commanded it. And you will have to be here!"

"Oh, Mother!" cried Miriam in desperation. "Why do we have such a tiresome, solemn old religion. I wish we had a religion like Zelda's. I went with her to the temple once. There was music and laughter, and dancing and flowers. Everybody was gay. Mother, why would I have to be here at the feast? Nobody would miss me if I stayed away."

"God would miss you!" said her mother awesomely. "Listen Miriam, we are going on a journey to-night! There is much to be done. It will take every minute to get ready."

"Oh, Mother! You've been talking about that journey a long time but we haven't gone yet. Why do you think we are going to-night? Zelda's father says that Pharaoh never intends to let us go, and he is close to the throne and ought to know. But anyway, even if we were allowed, Mother—why do *we* have to go with Israel? What do we want of a promised land? Why can't we stay right here? We have a nice home, and Zelda's father would always see that father had a good place. He might even get something to do in the palace. Why can't we stay and be Egyptians, and take the Egyptian gods for ours? I'd like that so much better, Mother!"

"Stop, Miriam!" said her mother sharply. "You are speaking blasphemies. Don't you know that our God is greater than all gods, that he is the *only true* God? Oh, my child! I have sinned! We were told to keep our children separate from all other peoples lest they forget their God who has covenanted with them. We are a chosen generation, a royal people! We should not mingle with the world. And I have let you grow up in close companionship with these Egyptian children! That of which we were warned has come to pass! My child is wanting to leave her God and serve those who are not gods at all! Oh, I have sinned!" she sobbed. "I thought there was no harm while you were little children, and you begged so hard to play with them! You were so little! I thought when you grew up you would learn to understand!"

She lifted her tear-wet eyes and spoke earnestly:

"Miriam, you must never speak this way again. It is sin!"

Miriam stood sullenly with downcast countenance still looking out the window toward Egypt.

"Well, anyhow, Joseph is going!" she pouted, "I heard him tell Zelda he would be over early to help Balthazar. They are going to the woods to get flowers to deck the house. And if Joseph goes I don't see why I can't go. He is only a year older than I am!"

The mother gave her a frightened look.

"He must not!" she said. "You don't understand. He

must help your father all day. And he must not be away from the house to-night! There is danger outside of our door."

Miriam gave her mother a quick startled look.

"What do you mean—danger?"

Her mother faced her earnestly, sadly.

"My dear, I haven't told you yet. I dreaded to bring you sorrow. Moses was here last night after you were asleep. He told your father that God is sending another plague—the last one. It is coming to-night. And then we are to go."

Miriam turned away impatiently.

"Oh, those horrid plagues!" she said angrily. "Zelda's father doesn't believe that Moses has anything to do with them, nor our God either. He says they just happen! But anyhow, Mother, those plagues don't come to Goshen anymore. Our cattle didn't die, and our men were not sick. When the dreadful hail storm came that spoiled all the gardens of Egypt it didn't touch us. Zelda's father says we just happened to be out of its path. And don't you remember when that awful darkness came, it was all light in Goshen?"

"But you, my child, are wanting to go out of Goshen to-night of all nights! Listen, my child, though it breaks your heart I must tell you. This plague is different from all others. Our God is passing through Egypt to-night to take the eldest son in every house. Only where He sees the sign of blood on the door will He pass over."

Miriam stood with suddenly blanched face, her hands clasped at her throat, a great fear growing in her eyes.

"Oh, Mother! Not *every* house, He wouldn't take Balthazar, would He?"

"He said every house," answered the mother sadly. "From the house of Pharaoh upon the throne, to the house of the maid behind the mill. Those were His very words."

"Oh, Mother, not Balthazar! Don't say He will take Balthazar! Why I was to dance with him to-night! And he is sending me flowers!"

Suddenly down the path came flying footsteps, a tap sounded upon the door, and Zelda, bright-faced and eager, burst into the room.

"Why don't you come, Miriam? You promised to be over long before this, and where is Joseph? Balthazar says the sun is high and the flowers will droop if they are not picked right away. Won't you call Joseph, and you both come at once?"

"I—can't come, Zelda—" murmured Miriam, white lipped, lifting eyes brimming with tears.

"You can't come? Why? What is the matter? You promised! I am depending on you."

"Zelda—something has happened! We have—a feast—to-night. I did not know about it before. And—we are going on a journey. But—oh—Zelda! It is something more than that! *Another plague is coming to-night.*"

"Another plague! How silly. I thought I had you all over that nonsense. How could you know a plague was coming, and why should that make any difference anyway? Are you a coward? We can take care of you if anything happens, though I don't believe it will."

"You don't understand, Zelda, this plague is different. Our God will pass through Egypt, and take the oldest son from every house unless the sign is over the door."

"How ridiculous!" laughed Zelda, with a sneer upon her lovely face. "My brother is well and strong. What do you think could happen to him between now and tomorrow morning? I told you all your family were superstitious, and now I know it. There! There is Joseph now in the yard with your father! I'm going out to make him come home with me. He has common sense. He won't be afraid to come."

She turned toward the door, her gaze still out the window, but suddenly stopped and drew back, her hands pressing at her throat.

"Oh," she cried out in fright, "what are they doing to that darling little white lamb? Isn't that the lamb your father had penned up, the one without a single spot? They're not going to *kill* it, are they? Oh, why does your mother let them do that? That darling little white lamb! I think they are cruel! Oh, see! There is blood!"

She pressed her fingers against her closed eyes:

"I cannot bear the sight of blood! It makes me feel faint!"

Then opening her eyes almost against her will she looked again:

"Why are they dipping that bunch of hyssop in the lamb's blood? Why are they doing that? Miriam, do you see? They are smearing it all over the door posts and over the lintel. Why doesn't your mother go out and stop them? What an awful thing to do! *Blood!*"

"It is our God's command," said Miriam solemnly. " 'When I see the blood, I will pass over you,' He said. It is to save my brother's life, Zelda."

Zelda looked at her scornfully.

"How could blood on a door post possibly save anybody?" she asked.

"You tell her, Mother," said Miriam, suddenly dropping into a chair, her head buried in her arms on the window sill, her shoulders shaking with sobs.

"Zelda, dear, it isn't that blood out there that saves Joseph's life. That blood is only a sign of our faith in a promise made long ago. Our God promised that some day He would send One who would be a lamb slain for the sins of the world, and that through His death all who believed would be saved. And so, when we put this blood on the door at His command to-night it is a sign that we trust in the blood of the Lamb that is to come. We are putting ourselves under the blood covenant, where we know we are safe. Do you understand?"

Then Miriam rose earnestly, with clasped hands and

pleading eyes looking into the angry startled face of her friend:

"Oh, Zelda, won't you go home right away and ask your father to kill a lamb and put the blood on your door? For perhaps God will see it and will pass over your house too, and your brother will be saved! Oh, won't you, Zelda?"

But Zelda met her with hard indignant eyes ablaze:

"What! Put blood on our door posts when I am going to have a dance? Why the guests would soil their beautiful garments! Now I know that you are not only superstitious but crazy! I hate you! I never want to see you anymore," and she dashed out of the door and down the path toward her home.

All day long as Miriam went about her work with tears raining down her white cheeks, her heart was aching with sorrow. As she prepared the bitter herbs for the feast, and made the unleavened bread, her eyes kept turning toward the lattice that looked over to Egypt, hoping against hope that perhaps after all Zelda had told her father. Perhaps before it was too late he might bring a lamb and put the needed sign upon his door also.

But the day went steadily on and she saw him not. The afternoon was on the wane. The house was full of the smell of roasting lamb. The clothing was stacked in convenient bundles for sudden going. Father and brother brought the sheep and cattle from the fields, and neighbors hurried by doing the same, their faces filled with grave apprehension.

Miriam, as she laid the table for the passover feast, kept looking out the window toward the house across the way. She saw the caterers arrive, and a little later the orchestra carrying their instruments. She choked back her tears and wished that she dared pray to the God whom she had neglected.

Lights were springing up in the big house. Guests in bright garments were arriving. Once she was sure she saw Balthazar standing in the open door, silhouetted against a blaze of light, directing the servant of a guest about his camel. Her heart leaped up with great longing to go and beg Balthazar to do something before it was too late! But it was too late now, with guests arriving over there for the dance, and the feast about to be served in her own home. Too late!

The passover feast was ready. The roasted lamb, with the bitter herbs and unleavened bread were set upon the table. The relatives had arrived who were to eat the lamb with them. They were all gathered about the solemn board, and Miriam's father lifted his hands to ask a blessing on the feast. Into the hush of that moment broke the music of the orchestra in the Egyptian house, and when Miriam lifted her eyes she could see the bright lights and the moving figures as the dancing began.

The night went on. The solemn feast came to a close. The midnight hour drew near and Israel waited with a hush of awe upon her homes.

Miriam suddenly glancing up at her brother Joseph, saw a look of wonder and exaltation upon his face such as she had never seen before. He was like one who has by some great act been set apart from others. There was a solemn beauty in his face that filled her with amazement.

Then her heart suddenly stood still. For the orchestra across the way crashed away into utter silence, and into the foreboding hush caused by its ceasing there came frightened voices, frantic calls, and she could see hurrying forms running hither and thither. A light sprang up on the housetop where she knew Balthazar had his room.

Then, into the listening night, there rose a cry of anguish such as never had been heard before, reaching from the house across the hedge to the next house, and the next house, and the next, all across the borders of Goshen, Egypt weeping for her sons whom the death angel had taken.

As they listened, with white faces lifted in awe and fear, there came a sound of footsteps flying down the path. The door burst open without ceremony, and Zelda burst in, her arms laden with bright silken garments, and her hands filled with chains and bracelets and jewels.

She rushed up to Miriam:

"Here! Take these, Miriam," she cried with anguish in her eyes. "Take them quick, and ask your father to get the people to go quickly! Oh, Miriam! My brother—is—DEAD!"

Then she turned and fled back to her desolated home. Solemnly the procession moved along. Out into the night went Miriam. Out under the far cold stars. Out toward the Red Sea and the wilderness, and a grave in the wilderness. Out following that pillar of fire!

Miriam in her place in the march was glad of the darkness to hide her tears. For every step of the way this one wish beat itself into her soul: "Oh, if I had only told them about our God before it was too late! If only I had *lived* the faith which my fathers believed! Ah, if I had *had* a faith of my own to live; I might have led them to believe also! But how could I teach them when instead I was walking in their ways?"

And then, suddenly, Miriam understood why God had commanded His people to be a separated people, His peculiar people, a royal generation, not expected to find their joy in the things of the world about them. It was because they had been called to higher, better things, promised by Him whose word could not be broken and the promise was sealed with blood!